KV-510-283

Aries the Ram

All About Aries

Aries is the first sign which starts the Zodiac, and that means an Aries girl always likes to get things going, and she loves coming first in everything! She's a winner because she's full of energy, she's got courage, and she isn't afraid to have a go at anything once. If you're an Aries, you're a straight-forward person, and you can't stand false people or hypocrites.

21st March - 20th April

You say what's on your mind, and you can be naive because you take others at face value and automatically trust them. But more than anything, an ARIES girl makes things happen, and without you, we'd all sit around and do nothing!

Bad Ram!

Aries girls are impatient and want things to happen immediately. So you can lose your temper quickly when you can't have what you want NOW! An Aries has got to learn that she's not the only person who matters, and getting your own way all the time isn't what life's all about. Aries also loves being WICKED and you sometimes do things at school just because your mates have dared you to do them. But who gets caught in the end? YOU, because people can read you like a book!

Talents and Hobbies

Aries girls are strong and tough and love working out. They are brilliant in the gym and great to have as top scorer on the netball or hockey team. You like boy's sports, especially football, but you dislike slow, fiddly hobbies. You'd prefer to go for a run round the block with the dog!

Home and School

An ARIES girl has to do things HER way, and she'll always rebel if she's told what to do, and how to do it, by parents or teachers. She gets nagged for being slap-dash and rushing through things, and then she loses her temper and shouts back. At home, her room looks like a bomb hit it and she's best with a room on her own because sharing with her would drive anyone mad!

Aries and Boys

You've always got on well with boys because you're a bit of a lad yourself, and you're a good buddy because you can be trusted. When you like a special boy you can't hide your feelings, but don't get TOO obvious or you'll frighten boys off! You also get bored quickly, so you get through lots of boys and never want to go steady.

The best boys for you are fire-signs like yourself, so try a Leo or Sagittarian. You can have big laughs with them and they'll admire your will-power. You get fed-up with gentle Cancer or Virgo lads, but if you want a challenge, choose an Aquarian. He'll tease you, but he'll really make you think about life and love!

Aries Girl

Find out how you get on with other starsigns, like your best friend or sister.

Aries the Ram
You become friends quickly but you fall out easily, too. You're never bored together and are always doing something.

Taurus the Bull
Taureans irritate you by being so slow but they are kind! The steady Bull also stops you from getting into too much trouble.

Gemini the Twins
A Gemini is chatty and cheeky and always makes you laugh, but a Twin can never keep up with you in sports and games.

Cancer the Crab
You often hurt their feelings and end up apologising all the time, but you can tell a gentle Crab anything and get sympathy.

Leo the Lion
You love Leos because they're such fun and have so many friends, but you don't like it when they're as bossy as you!

Virgo the Virgin
You admire how clever a Virgo is but you wish they weren't so quiet and would join in the fun more than they do.

Libra the Scales
You joke about how lazy a Libran can be and it's true, but you learn a lot from them about clothes, make–up, and true friendship.

Scorpio the Scorpion
You tell all your secrets but you can never work out what a Scorpion is up to, so you often feel cheated and your feelings get hurt.

Sagittarius the Archer
You get on really well together and the fun-loving Archer knows where the action is. You egg each other into doing outrageous things!

Capricorn the Goat
The Goat isn't a bit like you and often seems older and wiser! You can be a bit put off when they get serious and seem stuck-up.

Aquarius the Water Carrier
What a brilliant friend! The Water Carrier never bosses you around but sometimes you do worry that things get too wacky.

Pisces the Fishes
You get fed-up when a Pisces creates a muddle by day-dreaming. Without you, the Fish would never get anything done on time!

Taurus the Bull

All About Taurus

A Taurus girl is a real treasure because she is a good-natured sort who usually accepts what life brings her. She just gets on and makes the best of things. She comes through anything smiling because she's sensible and practical. She takes things one step at a time until she gets where she wants to be. If you're a Taurus, you are reliable and people trust you. You stick by those you love and you are very patient with babies and people who are upset or in trouble.

21st April - 20th May

You like to keep fit and love having body massages and lots of smelly stuff to make you feel fresh and bright. But more than anything, a Taurus girl is a nature lover, and you are at your happiest when you are in the garden or in the countryside, watching the animals and talking to the flowers and trees!

Bully Girl!

Taurus girls are determined and when you want something, you get stubborn and won't budge. Like the Bull, you get furious, lose your temper and charge around the house like a mad thing, thumping and banging things (and people!). Taureans also get possessive and when something belongs to YOU, such as a special toy or some fancy sweets, you want to keep them all to yourself. Learn to give and share more, and you'll get more back!

Talents and Hobbies

Taurus girls have a talent for making money, but they've also got a talent for spending it, so they don't get rich quick! For hobbies, you would rather play board games or chess than run the hundred metres, and you're good at pottery and baking cakes. You're also the girl with the golden voice, so you must SING!

Home and School

A Taurus girl never has time to finish her work, and gets behind because she works so carefully. Teachers like her grown-up attitude, and she does special jobs at lunch time, or for the school choir or band. At home, her room isn't spick and span but she hangs up her best clothes and looks after her favourite furry sweaters. She LOVES cushions and her room is so comfy, she has trouble getting out of bed in the morning!

Taurus and Boys

You're so pretty that boys think you're a knock-out. You need to know a boy for ages before you take him seriously, and you would like a steady boyfriend. If you find one, don't treat him as if he's all yours, or you'll frighten him off by being possessive.

The best boys for you are earth signs like yourself, so try a Virgo or Capricorn. You feel safe with them because they are genuine. Aries and Sagittarian boys can be scary because they seem to be laughing at you. So if you want a lad to laugh WITH, choose a Pisces. He will make sure you never get stuck in a rut.

Taurus Girl

Find out how you get on with other starsigns, like your best friend or sister.

Aries the Ram
The Ram is honest and pushes you into doing things you wouldn't normally do. But they can do stupid things that get you in trouble.

Taurus the Bull
You like the same things but neither of you talks much and slobbing in front of the TV with pop and crisps makes you both bored!

Gemini the Twins
You like the Twins because they tell jokes about wicked things, but they let you down sometimes by not turning up.

Cancer the Crab
You get on brilliantly and love going to town, gossiping in burger bars. You tell each other everything about your families - and boys!

Leo the Lion
You make the Lions furious because they can't boss you around. They respect you, and you secretly admire them.

Virgo the Virgin
Virgos can read you like a book. They give you good advice and you have a laugh when you're sarcastic with each other.

Libra the Scales
You love trying on the latest fashions and each other's make-up. But they keep changing their minds, so it takes ages to go anywhere!

Scorpio the Scorpion
You can't ignore each other but when you are both so proud and wilful, it's sometimes hard for you to get along. Be more tolerant!

Sagittarius the Archer
You think the Archer clowns about too much and they are always cadging money and sweets, but sometimes they cheer you up.

Capricorn the Goat
You love being around each other and time flies at each other's houses, or just talking about life and love. Definitely best buddies!

Aquarius the Water Carrier
You like having a good argument together about God, the universe and what's right and wrong. But neither of you ever wins!

Pisces the Fishes
You talk a lot and it's good to know you're always there for each other. But if you both keep guzzling chocolate, you'll get the zits!

The Elements

Each star sign belongs to one of the elements, FIRE, EARTH, AIR and WATER. Find your element here.

FIRE GIRLS
Aries, Leo, Sagittarius

Fire girls love life, they burst with energy and throw themselves into one adventure after another with oodles of enthusiasm. If you're a fire girl, you're popular because you are self-confident and fun to be with. But remember, fire can be dangerous and you sometimes get into awkward situations, or you become too hot to handle. Burn steadily, and you'll burn brightly!

EARTH GIRLS
Taurus, Virgo, Capricorn

Earth girls have lots of common sense, they know how to do things and they work and practise happily for hours to make the best of their talents. If you're an earth girl, you are ambitious and reliable, and you like to be organised, so don't get phased by the razzle-dazzle of other girls. But remember, earth can get bogged down, so never take too many worries on yourself. Climb your mountains steadily, and you'll get to the top!

AIR GIRLS
Gemini, Libra, Aquarius

Air sign girls are full of ideas, always reading and listening to music, eager to tell everyone about the fascinating information they come across. If you're an air girl, you are intelligent and clever with words, and you care about humanity all over the world. But remember, air can turn into strong gales and blow everything down. So be gentle when you're putting ideas across, and you'll breeze through life!

WATER GIRLS
Cancer, Scorpio, Pisces

Water sign girls have strong likes and dislikes, they brim with emotions and they are sympathetic and responsive to the people around them. If you're a water girl, you like being close to those you love, and you enjoy having a heart-to-heart so you get to the bottom of each other's problems. But remember, water can make things soppy, so don't be too sentimental and you'll swim happily through life!

Gemini the Twins

All About Gemini

Gemini is the sign of the Twins, and that means a Gemini girl is always in two minds and keeps chopping and changing her ideas about everything. She's a curiosity cat, a real live wire who hates to be bored. If you're a Gemini, you are especially good with words and love to communicate and make connections, so you're happy when you're chatting on the phone, gossiping with friends or writing letters.

You are also really quick at what you do and that's because you skim the surface, like a stone over water, picking up bits of information as you go along. The intelligent and friendly spark in your eyes shows that you are interested in everyone and everything around you - and that's what makes everyone interested in YOU!

Talkative Twin

Gemini girls are so bright and quick, they can put down slow people and think they are boring. A Gemini has got to learn to appreciate other people's strengths and talents, and then she will have more understanding of other people and what makes them tick. Geminis can also get in trouble when they tell fibs and pull tricks on people, and that's usually because the Twins want two opposite things, and you don't like to admit it. Try hard to tell the truth - even if you aren't sure what it is!

Talents and Hobbies

Gemini girls are clever and have so many talents and hobbies, it's difficult to know which ones to concentrate on. You love reading your books and mags, or playing on the computer, and you're brilliant at crosswords and Scrabble. As long as you have at least two things to do, you're happy!

Home and School

A Gemini girl must have plenty of books and magazines lying around and has posters and newspaper cuttings all over the walls of her room which she changes all the time. At school she does her homework at the last minute and still gets good marks, and she does really well in foreign languages. She's terrible to sit next to and often gets told off for talking too much, but she usually gets round the teachers by making them laugh.

Gemini and Boys

You're never short of chat-up lines with boys
and they love you because you're such fun
and you don't take anything too seriously. You
are difficult to pin down and you probably
have a reputation for being a flirt, and playing
two boys off against each other. Naughty!

The best boys for you are air signs like
yourself, so try an Aquarian or Libran. You
can talk to them for hours, especially about
music, and they love your ideas and witty
comments. You're not happy around fussy
Virgo boys or soppy, romantic Pisceans. If you
really want thrills and spills, pick an Aries.
He's pushy, but he's never boring!

Gemini Girl

Find out how you get on with other starsigns, like your best friend or sister.

Aries the Ram
The Ram is bossy but lots of fun and you love the way they are always ready to go on the spur of the moment.

Taurus the Bull
Taureans bore you when they get stuck in a rut or are slow. They only get jokes hours later. But the Bull always has the best sweets.

Gemini the Twins
You're like two peas in a pod. You're always quarrelling and everyone else thinks you mean it, but you're just playing.

Cancer the Crab
Cancerians make you feel restless because they don't come to the point. They ARE kind, but they're always scared about stupid things.

Leo the Lion
You can catch Leos out and take the mickey out of their airs and graces. But the Lion is a great mate and you have lots of fun together.

Virgo the Virgin
Virgos are clever and quick, but you get fed-up when they fuss over things. But when you plot together, you can be very mischievous.

♊

Libra the Scales
Librans can be too girly for you. They don't like getting their clothes messed up, but they do know a lot about make-up and fashion.

Scorpio the Scorpion
You love solving puzzles together and getting the low-down on others. You admire the way the Scorpion can get to the bottom of things.

Sagittarius the Archer
The Archer is really popular but you're not too keen on her sporty side. Sagittarians never fib and always want you to tell the truth!

Capricorn the Goat
You're about the only one who appreciates a Capricorn's odd sense of humour but in the end, the Goat can be too serious for you.

Aquarius the Water Carrier
You love playing on computers or musical instruments together. The Water Carrier is up to date with the latest ideas and information.

Pisces the Fishes
A Piscean's feelings can be hurt if you criticise what she has made or written. You love their gentleness, even if you don't always show it.

Zodiac Dads

What do the stars say about your Dad? Know his plus points and why he's so special.

Aries Dad
He rushes around, starting jobs he never finishes. He shouts a lot but he smiles a lot, too. He loves his car - and YOU!

Taurus Dad
He's slow and stubborn and he loves his food. But he's always there with a big hug for you when you need it.

Gemini Dad
He's often reading the papers or on the phone. He has nicknames for everyone and makes you laugh with all his silly voices.

Cancer Dad
He's a big softie who loves to be at home, and he's the only one that gets his jokes, But deep down, he understands you more than anyone.

Leo Dad
What a show off! He loves holidays and parties and he's so proud of you, he boasts about you to everyone. Embarrassing!

Virgo Dad
He works hard and he's kind. He doesn't shout or get bossy, except when he wants to see your report. He loves pets as much as you.

Libra Dad

He's gentle and funny, and he loves his sweets and puddings. He wants you to enjoy life and not take things too seriously.

Scorpio Dad

He tells the best stories and loves to show you how things work, especially in nature. He's good with secrets and always keeps them.

Sagittarius Dad

He plays silly, practical jokes and he exaggerates about everything. He loves being outdoors and always wants to go camping.

Capricorn Dad

He's quite strict and doesn't like being shown-up in public. He loves special Saturday treats. Tweak his nose if he gets too serious.

Aquarius Dad

He loves gadgets and new inventions. He has lots of plans to change the world, but he can't even put his socks on properly.

Pisces Dad

He loves taking you to the movies and he's a great dancer. He's probably too soft on you for your own good!

Cancer the Crab

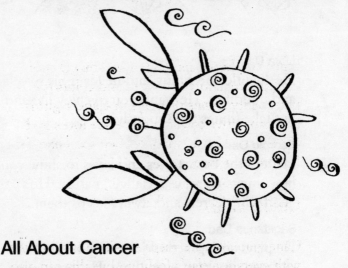

All About Cancer

The Cancer girl is sensitive and thoughtful. She has a vivid imagination and is happy either playing for hours on her own, or being the centre of attention by making everyone laugh with her impersonations of the family. If you are a Cancerian, you have a wonderful memory and always remember birthdays and important dates. But you ARE shy, and you can be moody, so it takes you a long time to feel secure with new people. Sometimes you dread that others will laugh at your ideas and feelings.

21st June - 22nd July

Once you know someone well you get more confidence, and your warm and colourful personality shines through. A Cancer girl is also protective towards those she loves and she'll have a go at anyone when someone she is close to is threatened.

Crusty Crab

Cancerian girls are mega sensitive and in tune with everyone else's feelings, but this can also get them down and they become too moody for their own good. When a Cancerian is feeling low, she can't hide it but she hates to be seen that way. Instead of retreating into your shell, try to lighten up and shake yourself out of feeling negative by getting out of the house. Moods are always shifting and changing, so never let yourself get stuck by being a silent Crab - SPEAK to the people you love, and things will miraculously change!

Talents and Hobbies

Cancer girls have a knack with food and love helping out in the kitchen. You're good at observing everything tiny and delicate, and you love nature and small animals. You like to play quietly and don't enjoy boisterous games. You've got a flare for photography, and you write great stories.

 ## Home and School

A Cancer girl finds it difficult to throw anything away so her room is filled with old toys, teddy bears and favourite clothes she can't bear to part with. She also has a KEEP OUT! drawer for her lockable diary and special photos. At school she takes it to heart when a teacher tells her off so she tries to be good to avoid conflict. She's good with children and loves helping out with smaller pupils, and she makes the best ever baby-sitter.

Cancer and Boys

You have to know a boy well before you let him know you like him, so you hide your feelings for months. Boys love your gentleness and feel safe telling you their secrets because they know you won't make fun of them. You can get easily hurt and sometimes a stupid boy upsets you by saying cruel things, but he just doesn't understand you.

The best boys for you are water signs like yourself, Scorpio or Pisces. They understand your moods and you'll fall for their romantic stories. Aries and Aquarius are too hurtful and impatient, so if you want a steady boyfriend, choose a Taurus. He will NEVER let you down!

Cancer Girl

Find out how you get on with other starsigns, like your best friend or sister.

Aries the Ram
You like them because they are direct and don't mess about, but they're scary when they lose their temper and shout.

Taurus the Bull
The Bull makes you feel safe and secure and is always ready with a hug and a smile when you're feeling down.

Gemini the Twins
You find the Twins irritating as they change their minds. But they are good company and you get to know lots of people through them.

Cancer the Crab
They understand you but sometimes it feels as if nothing much is happening, and you end up at each other's houses every weekend.

Leo the Lion
Leos buy brilliant presents and make a fuss of you but they have so many friends, you can feel left out and start to lose your confidence.

Virgo the Virgin
You love the way Virgos help you to look pretty and tidy but they are hurtful when they feel you're getting at them.

Libra the Scales

You sometimes feel that Librans come from a different planet. They don't show their feelings very often, and you find that odd.

Scorpio the Scorpion

You think Scorpios are deep and interesting. They get you to try new things. They don't care about popularity and that worries you.

Sagittarius the Archer

You love the way the Archer never worries about anything. Their confidence rubs off on you and turns you into Supergirl!

Capricorn the Goat

A Capricorn always takes you seriously if you've a problem. The Goat gives you good advice, but sometimes thinks you're too soft!

Aquarius the Water Carrier

You love exploring together but you find an Aquarian's ideas a bit odd. They take things too lightly and you don't feel understood.

Pisces the Fishes

They're a good friend and never say anything hurtful or cruel. You both love playing with animals, and you're both the weepy type!

Zodiac Mums

What kind of person is your mum?
Here's why she is the BEST mum in the world!

Aries Mum

She's bossy, quick tempered, and loves to keep fit! But she gives you freedom, and she stands up for you against ANYBODY!

Taurus Mum

She's patient and steady, and helps you with clothes. She loves sun-bathing and gardening, she's a great cook and feeds you well.

Gemini Mum

She's not home much and when she is, she's always talking and arguing! She's smart, and encourages you to do homework.

Cancer Mum

She's tidy and encourages you to bring friends home. But she'll show them photos of you, aged three, and cry at sad films.

Leo Mum

She's glamorous and confident, and always bossing everyone. She loves holidays and gives you great pressies as she's so proud of you.

Virgo Mum

She bustles around the house and she wants you to be tidy, clean and healthy. She knows exactly what to do about your problems.

Libra Mum
She can persuade anyone into anything! She treats all her kids the same, and never gets upset. She likes everyone to have a good time.

Scorpio Mum
She's strict but she understands your moods. She loves her astrology and mysteries, and she teaches you to question everything!

Sagittarius Mum
She loves travelling, dogs and horses. She can't cook but enjoys barbecues. She's like a big kid herself, so she's easy to get round!

Capricorn Mum
She doesn't get your jokes, but she's ambitious for you. She's not the cuddly sort, but she cares about you more than anything.

Aquarius Mum
She's got strong beliefs and is quite trendy. She encourages you to be independent and she gets on well with your friends.

Pisces Mum
She day-dreams about winning the lottery, and is very absent-minded. But she'll do ANYTHING for you.

Leo the Lion

All about Leo

Leo the Lion is the king of the jungle, and that means a Leo girl is a courageous, proud lioness, full of colour and confidence. She's a winner because she loves life and believes in herself, and she's a generous, giving person who wants everyone to shine like she does. If you're a Leo, you've also got a creative talent which you should make the most of, especially if it means putting on a show or making things.

23rd July - 22nd August

You like going out and having a good time, and you believe that the more you put into something, the more you get out of it. But more than anything, Leo is a BOSS, and because she is such a brill leader and organiser, she brings out the best in others and everyone is happy to follow her!

Bossy Boots!

Leo girls get too cocky for their own good sometimes, showing off and being loud and jokey. They put themselves first and don't stop to think about how other people feel about what they're doing. A Leo has to learn that if she's bossy or stuck-up, she won't be a popular girl! Leos also love life to be dramatic and eventful, but if the big cats could just purr along and enjoy little, everyday things, they would be loved by everyone!

Talents and Hobbies

Leo girls are bursting with creative energy. Drama brings out their talents but they also love art, design and making jewellery. They get a thrill from competitions but they're not good at team sports because they always want the ball! Their absolutely favourite thing is SUN-BATHING. Like cats, they doze in the sun for hours!

Home and School

A Leo girl likes to be top of the class but she only works when she likes a subject, such as English or Art, and won't even try otherwise. She's popular with other girls and pulls hilarious jokes on the teachers to make them mad. At home, her room is a palace with pressies and ornaments on show, including her old teddy! She likes bright, sunny colours for her quilt but her favourite thing is a white, fluffy rug to squiggle her tootsies in!

Leo and Boys

You're so popular with boys, you probably had your first boyfriend when you were three! You get a buzz when a boy admires you and you're not frightened to let him know you like him. You're faithful and would ditch a boy immediately if he two-timed you.

The best boys for you are fire signs like yourself, so try an Aries or Sagittarian. They're action lads who will take you to new places. You feel trapped by Pisces and Capricorn boys, so for a good match, choose a Libran. You can boss him about, and he'll love you for it even more!

Leo Girl

Find out how you get on with other starsigns, like your best friend or sister.

Aries the Ram
You and the Ram are always up to something outrageous! You're full of life, but you're both bossy madams!

Taurus the Bull
You love the Bull's good taste and brill clothes but you get tired of being the life and soul while they just tag along.

Gemini the Twins
The dynamic duo! The Twins bring out the show-off in you. You trek around together, checking out the latest shops and hang-outs.

Cancer the Crab
The Crabs never say directly what they want, and that brings out your bossy side. You are always having to tell them what to do!

Leo the Lion
You're both lively and dramatic but Lions compete with each other to be leader of the pack. It can be a fight to the end!

Virgo the Virgin
You admire that Virgos get things done and finish jobs they have started, but they are SO helpful, it's easy to treat one like your slave!

Libra the Scales
You talk for hours about love and boys, but when it comes to actually chatting them up, unlike you, she's all talk.

Scorpio the Scorpion
As you're so open, it's hard to trust secretive Scorpios. You never know what they're up to, and they always think you're mysterious too!

Sagittarius the Archer
You are both adventurous and dream of being rich, famous, and travelling round the world. Dream on ... and have lots of laughs together!

Capricorn the Goat
You're slightly scared of them because they act as if they know everything. But you both want to be Prime Minister when you're older.

Aquarius the Water Carrier
They challenge you to defend the things you really believe in, but you like arguing with them and admire their brainy ideas.

Pisces the Fishes
You both enjoy acting and films, but you want to organise them, and don't realise they like swimming along in their own muddled way!

Fashion and Jewellery

What clothes and jewellery suit your star sign?

Aries
Bright colours are best but keep things simple. You're a tomboy who loves leggings, but dangly earrings make you mega attractive.

Taurus
Flowery patterns and dresses suit you, and hairbands and ribbons make you look pretty. Your favourite jewellery is always a necklace.

Gemini
T-shirts are best, especially if they're stripey. Try mixing colours that aren't supposed to go together, and wear clinky bangles or bracelets.

Cancer
Snug jumpers and velvety skirts are for you. Your favourite thing is a silver locket with a photo inside, probably of your family.

Leo
Sunshine colours make you feel good, and you love fancy buttons that button up the back. Feel swanky and wear REAL gold!

Virgo
Cardigans and jumpers make you feel at home and you love comfy shoes, especially brown ones. Delicate rings show off your hands.

Libra

You like the latest fashions, but pretty, light materials always suit you. You look great in a belt with a beautiful buckle.

Scorpio

Exotic clothes from the East in red or purple suit you, and dark colours make you mysterious. Chunky rings are also your style.

Sagittarius

You like tracksuits and jeans as they're quick and easy, even if Mum thinks you look scruffy. But add beads and wristbands to look glam.

Capricorn

You love snug coats or jackets, but be daring and wear colourful tights or socks. Your fave jewellery is something someone gave you.

Aquarius

Long skirts, zany leggings and clumpy boots make you feel brilliant. Anything electric blue attracts you, and you love beads and crystals.

Pisces

You go for comfy trousers and jumpers or pretty dresses, depending on your mood. Seahorse or fishy jewellery brings you luck.

Virgo the Virgin

All About Virgo

A Virgo girl is practical, clever and a really hard worker. She's always willing to lend a helping hand and doesn't mind missing out on attention or glamour, so long as she knows she's done her best. If you're a Virgo, you don't show off or try too hard to be popular because you know that you have all the friends you need, and those lucky people are hand-picked and special. You're not noisy and rough like some girls and you're always stylish with good taste in clothes and jewellery.

23rd August - 22nd September

You like to look neat and tidy. That's because you're choosy, and you don't rush into anything before having a long, hard think. You aim for perfection and hate it when you make a mistake, or get blamed for something, especially when you've done your best. You're careful in what you say and do, about your health and what you eat, and that makes you a very wise girl indeed!

Vexing Virgo

Virgo girls win first prize at worrying! Fretting about silly little details means it takes you twice as long to get anything done. Learn to be less fussy. You criticise others but won't put up with anyone moaning at you. And please, let someone else in the bathroom! You like to be so clean and well-scrubbed, you spend hours soaking in the tub!

Talents and Hobbies

Virgos are good with their hands and want to keep busy. You like being in the garden growing vegetables, and you love the birds and squirrels in the countryside. You're brill at sewing and would like to make your own clothes. You're also a Miss Fix-It and enjoy repairing anything broken, but most of all, you LOVE encyclopaedias and could read them forever!

Home and School

Virgo girls are good at school work and their homework is neat, but it takes them ages to finish it because they want to be right. Strangely, unless you share, your room is often a mess because it's the only place you can let things slide. Your teachers and parents give you a lot of responsibility for your age and you're probably a prefect or monitor, but TELL them if they're expecting too much from you!

Virgos and Boys

You get noticed by all the boys, even though you never make the first move and act independently, as if you're not bothered. They like your mysterious manner and want to find out more about you. If you show lads how quick and funny you are, and don't criticise their clothes or attitude, you'll be a big hit with them.

The boys that suit you best are the other earth signs, Capricorn and Taurus. They don't get carried away with daft ideas. Geminis and Sagittarians get on your nerves with their noise and jokes, but a Scorpio intrigues you and you want to find out his secrets!

Virgo Girl

Find out how you get on with other starsigns, like your best friend or sister.

Aries the Ram
An Aries is quick and sparky but sometimes is too slap-dash for you. You can both be bad tempered but she never bears you a grudge.

Taurus the Bull
You'll be friends for years because Taureans are always there when you need them, and they find it funny when you pull their leg.

Gemini the Twins
They've always got something interesting to say and they know everything that's going on, but the Twins can be too noisy for you.

Cancer the Crab
You love the way the kind Crab calms you down and is a good listener, but you can't bear their sulks and sudden moods.

Leo the Lion
You do all the work while Leo swans around, showing off and taking the credit. They'll like you more if you say no sometimes.

Virgo the Virgin
Don't tell each other ALL your faults, or you'll nag each other silly! You both love looking after animals.

Libra the Scales
Librans are so pretty and ladylike you wish you could be like them, but their laziness is too much sometimes.

Scorpio the Scorpion
Scorpios know what matters and they're different to anyone else you know. But they get their own back if you put them down!

Sagittarius the Archer
You find them messy and untidy and wonder how they get away with outrageous things, but they spur you to travel and think big.

Capricorn the Goat
They are sensible and won't let you fret about unimportant things. You admire their control and the calm way they handle things.

Aquarius the Water Carrier
You're both cool and don't show your feelings easily, but you get along because both of you are also strong-minded and independent.

Pisces the Fishes
You're like chalk and cheese but you balance each other out. You share their dreams and you help them to make dreams come true!

Zodiac things

Each starsign is linked to all kinds of things in your life.
Find out which things are best for your sign.

Aries
Your lucky day is TUESDAY, your colour is RED, your metal is IRON, and your precious stone is GARNET. Your HEAD is your special zodiac body part, and your foods are SPICES, CURRY and GINGER.

Taurus
Your lucky day is FRIDAY, your colour is GREEN, your metal is BRASS, and your precious stone is JADE. Your NECK and THROAT are special, and your foods are HONEY and CREAM.

Gemini
Your lucky day is WEDNESDAY, your colour is YELLOW, your metal is QUICKSILVER, and your stone is TOPAZ. Your HANDS and ARMS are special, and your foods are BEANS and LIQUORICE.

Cancer
Your lucky day is MONDAY, your colour is CREAM, your metal is SILVER, and your precious stone is PEARL. Your CHEST AND TUMMY are special and your foods are CABBAGE and MELONS.

Leo
Your lucky day is SUNDAY, your colour is SCARLET, your metal is GOLD, and your precious stone is DIAMOND. Your HEART is special and your foods are ORANGES and LEMONS.

Virgo
Your lucky day is WEDNESDAY, your colours are BROWN and LILAC, your metal is QUICKSILVER, and your stone is TOPAZ. Your INTESTINES are special and your foods are TREACLE and WALNUTS.

Libra

Your lucky day is FRIDAY, your colour is BLUE-GREY, your metal is COPPER, and your precious stones are OPAL and JADE. Your WAIST and KIDNEYS are special and your foods are APPLES and PLUMS.

Scorpio

Your lucky day is TUESDAY, your colours are WINE and PLUM, your metal is IRON, and your stones are BLOODSTONE and RUBY. Your PRIVATE BITS are special, and your foods are PEPPERS and GARLIC.

Sagittarius

Your lucky day is THURSDAY, your colour is PURPLE, your metal is TIN, and your precious stone is EMERALD. Your HIPS and THIGHS are special, and your foods are STRAWBERRIES and CHERRIES.

Capricorn

Your lucky day is SATURDAY, your colours are BLACK and INDIGO, your metal is LEAD, and your precious stone is JET. Your KNEES and TEETH are special, and your foods are SPINACH and PARSNIPS.

Aquarius

Your lucky day is SATURDAY, your colour is BLUE, your metal is URANIUM, and your precious stone is SAPPHIRE. Your ANKLES are special and your foods are MUESLI and CHRISTMAS CAKE.

Pisces

Your lucky day is THURSDAY, your colour is SEA-GREEN, your metal is TIN, and your precious stone is AMETHYST. Your FEET are special, and your foods are OLIVES and PASTA.

Libra the Scales

All about Libra

Libra the Scales is the only star sign which has an object, instead of an animal or person, as its picture. This means that a Libran girl is good at weighing things up logically, balancing different points of view and coming to a fair decision. If you're a Libran, you are tolerant and although you seem to agree with everyone, in the end you will argue like a tiger if you think something is wrong and should be put right.

Most of the time, though, you want people to be friends and to live in peace and harmony. More than anything, a Libran girl is looking for someone to love. She doesn't like being on her own and whether it's a brother or sister, a boy or her fave pooch, she's GOT to have someone to share everything with.

Tipping the Scales

Libran girls can get lazy and shy away from hard work or difficult challenges, so they give up easily or change their mind and come up with excuses or some other hair-brained scheme. A Libran has got to realise that other people won't do all the unpleasant chores for her which she dislikes doing. She also tries to be friends with everyone, but she can't please ALL of the people ALL of the time. So finish what you start, Libra, and at least you'll please somebody!

Talents and Hobbies

Libran girls are mega persuasive and can convince anyone of anything, and they also have a knack of making people feel better. They cheer everyone up by writing songs, playing music, painting pictures and enjoying all the art and culture that parents and teachers take them to see. They love fashion but their biggest hobby is definitely BOYS!

Home & School

A Libran girl often gets "could try harder" from teachers at school but she loves debates and class discussions. At home she wants everything to be pleasant and colourful, but she has piles of books and mags in her room and her clothes end up where she drops them. She's so busy trying out new hairstyles in the mirror, or waiting for her nail varnish to dry, she doesn't have time to tidy up!

Libra and Boys

You're a girly-girl who likes to look good and you love it when boys stare at you and find you attractive. You flirt with any lad and fall in love at least twice a week! Sometimes you try too hard to please a boy but the more strong-willed you are, the more he will respect you.

The best boys for you are air signs like yourself, so try a Gemini or an Aquarian. You share ideas and music with them, and they laugh at the same things as you. Taureans and Scorpios can sometimes bully you, so if you want a lad who gives you space to be yourself, choose a Sagittarian. He's a flirt, but so are you!

Libra Girl

Find out how you get on with other starsigns, like your best friend or sister.

Aries the Ram
You're opposites, but opposites attract! You love the way the Rams act on impulse, but you should stop them, sometimes!

Taurus the Bull
You both enjoy painting, drawing and making things and you want others to join in, but the Bull is happier with just the two of you.

Gemini the Twins
Everyone laughs when you and the Twins do impersonations. You get along brilliantly and always find new things to do.

Cancer the Crab
They take everything you say seriously, even when you're thinking out loud. They can be annoying when they refuse to work things out.

Leo the Lion
Life is a rave with you and the Lions. YOU have fab ideas and THEY are brave enough, and daft enough, to try them out!

Virgo the Virgin
You love that a Virgo looks neat and perfect in delicate colours and patterns. But you disappear when they nag you to work harder!

Libra the Scales
You agree on lots of things, and talk for hours about your likes and dislikes. But then you take hours to decide where to go, and when!

Scorpio the Scorpion
You think they don't take you seriously, and you don't like the way they probe into your private things. You avoid them if you can.

Sagittarius the Archer
You love the Archer's generosity, and the way they include you in their parties, games and sports, especially when they go horse riding.

Capricorn the Goat
They help you make the right choices, especially with school work. They know how to get their own way with parents, too!

Aquarius the Water Carrier
You love each other to bits but you're both really scatty. You're both so busy yakking that you forget the time, walk into lamp-posts etc.!

Pisces the Fishes
You might know lots of Pisceans and at first you get along well, but you can get them to do anything and then you don't respect them!

The Planets

Your star sign is linked to one or two planets. Know your strengths and weaknesses through the planets.

Aries
Red Mars makes you energetic and forceful. Your strength is your will-power and ability to fight. But don't be too bolshie and pushy!

Taurus
Beautiful Venus makes you loving and friendly. Your strength is to get along with others. But don't fall for every boy you know!

Gemini
Speedy Mercury makes you talkative and intelligent. Your strength is your quick wit. But don't be a blabbermouth or gossip.

Cancer
The changeable Moon makes you sensitive. Your strength is your imagination and caring for others. But don't be too moody or clingy!

Leo
The bright Sun makes you creative and confident. Your strength is being an organiser and a leader. But don't show-off too much!

Virgo
Speedy Mercury makes you studious and mischievous. You are intelligent and can work things out, but don't be a cunning little minx!

Libra
Beautiful Venus makes you peaceful and charming. Your strength is you can put wrong things right again. But don't be too airy-fairy!

Scorpio
Mars makes you strong-willed, and Pluto makes you powerful. You are determined to see things through. But don't be a tyrant!

Sagittarius
Giant Jupiter makes you freedom-loving and adventurous. You are enthusiastic and have big dreams. But don't be too big-headed!

Capricorn
Saturn makes you ambitious and disciplined. You do your duty, and you can handle difficulties but don't be too strict on yourself!

Aquarius
Saturn makes you serious and thoughtful, but Uranus makes you rebellious. You have strong opinions, but try to see the funny side of life!

Pisces
Jupiter makes you optimistic, and Neptune gives you dreams of the future. You're imaginative, but don't day-dream too much!

Scorpio the Scorpion

All About Scorpio

The Scorpio girl is special - and she knows it!
She stands out because of her mysterious and
intense mood which gives her a magnetic
attraction. If you're a Scorpio, you are a very
strong-willed person with a sense of your own
power. You know what you like and more
important, what you DON'T like, and this
makes you confident and certain about most
things. You feel passionately about all the
world's troubles, especially wars and famines,
and you want to improve things around you
and make them better.

You can always spot when someone is hiding something or they are secretly unhappy, and that gives you an advantage over other people. You love to delve into anything secret and hidden, and you're fascinated by people's minds and what makes them tick. If anyone can get to the bottom of things, a Scorpio can!

Scorpio Sting

Scorpio girls, like the Scorpion, DO have a sting in their tails and they have to watch how they use such a powerful weapon. You can put other girls down and be really horrible to them when you're using that sting, usually because you are jealous of them. No-one probably realises how strongly you feel because you hide your upsets and moods well. But try to share your thoughts and feelings - even the bad ones - and you'll find the world an easier place to live in.

Talents and Hobbies

Scorpio girls are great swimmers and divers, and brilliant detectives. They love reading who-dunnits, ghost stories and tales of Merlin the Magician. You're also interested in medicine and often seem to know when something's wrong. You love taking things apart to find out how they work, and that makes you unpopular with Mum and Dad!

Home and School

Your room is YOURS and you hate anyone going in without your knowledge, so you set traps for them! You have secret hiding places and love to squirrel away where no one can find you. At school you get in trouble by sticking up for your mates and getting punished, even though you haven't done anything wrong. You love playing around with test-tubes and chemicals and you're good at nature subjects.

Scorpio and Boys

You're never short of admirers and boys find you sexy when you stare at them with your magnetic eyes. You always want the boy who you can't have because you can't resist a challenge. You can be hurtful if a boy lets you down and when you REALLY like a lad, you get jealous and obsessed.

The boys who suit you best are Cancer and Pisces because they are water signs, too. They are as passionate about life as you. Keep away from Aquarians or Leos or you'll be forever fighting, but if you want a loyal boyfriend, choose a Taurus. You're opposites, and as you know from science, opposites attract!

Scorpio Girl

Find out how you get on with other starsigns, like your best friend or sister.

Aries the Ram
You can't believe what they come out with and Rams can never keep a secret, but you love their fiery, dare-devil energy.

Taurus the Bull
The Bull understands your stormy moods without getting upset, and they help you work out solutions to your problems.

Gemini the Twins
You wish Geminis didn't chat so much but you like their jokiness. And THEIR questions make YOU question your own beliefs.

Cancer the Crab
Cancerians are too worried about what their Mums and Dads might think, but the Crab is a good friend, and always on your side.

Leo the Lion
The Lion is far too bossy for you and has to be the centre of attention. They stick up for their friends, but you often end up clashing.

Virgo the Virgin
They are careful and love small, delicate things. You like a Virgo's speed and neatness, and they are a big help with homework.

Libra the Scales
Librans annoy you when they can't make up their minds. But you can boss them around and usually get them to do what you want.

Scorpio the Scorpion
You find it difficult to trust another Scorpion but once you do, you become best buddies, sharing everything, even clothes and lipstick.

Sagittarius the Archer
The Archer is different to you and is not very serious. They clown around which makes you laugh at first, but it soon gets boring.

Capricorn the Goat
You work well together at school and Goats always stick by their word. But you can argue with each other about who's in charge!

Aquarius the Water Carrier
You don't have much in common but you both like joining clubs and societies. You enjoy arguing about the state of the world.

Pisces the Fishes
Pisceans bring out the best in you and make you feel so safe that you tell them

Jobs and Careers

What are you good at and what job will make you happy?

Aries
You learn fast when you're interested, but you're an action girl who dislikes fussy details.
Army, police, fire brigade, sportswoman.

Taurus
You stick at things and never let anyone down. You love clothes, money and nature!
Bank manager, gardener, cook, singer.

Gemini
You love to gossip, especially on the phone. You like things to be different every day.
Journalist, computer expert, writer, secretary.

Cancer
You are gentle and caring, friends always ask your advice. You bring out the best in people.
Nursery teacher, social worker, personnel.

Leo
You are very confident and make others feel organised and talented, but you're the boss!
Actress, business woman, teacher, manager.

Virgo
You like to feel useful and prefer to work behind the scenes, supporting other people.
Vet, nurse, secretary, crafts and pottery.

Libra

You're good at talking to people and like making everything around you beautiful.
Counsellor, dress designer, artist, florist.

Scorpio

You're tough and don't mind being shouted at, and you're brilliant at keeping secrets.
Doctor, psychologist, detective, bus driver.

Sagittarius

You've got a sense of adventure and you love horses, foreign countries, and crime stories.
Travel agent, sportswoman, lawyer.

Capricorn

You work really hard and like people to know how much you've done. You're very reliable.
Police, politics, history teacher, company boss.

Aquarius

You care about people and love new ideas. You want to make the world a better place.
Social worker, scientist, computers, media.

Pisces

You have a brilliant imagination. You're good at pretending and you want to save the world!
Actress, dancer, film-maker, charity worker.

Sagittarius the Archer

All About Sagittarius

A Sagittarian girl always looks on the bright side of life and tries to make the best of any situation. She is full of energy and enthusiasm and has a wonderful sense of fun, clowning about and making everyone laugh with her antics. But there's also a religious side to her and she loves reading stories about religious people and events. If you're a Sagittarian, you have to feel free to do your own thing. You dislike rules and people in authority telling you what to do.

You hate being cooped up indoors and there's nothing you like better than chasing around outside. You are also very open and frank and believe in telling the truth. You speak your mind and can't see the point in having secrets. If only there were more people like you!

Rotten Shot!

Sagittarian girls tend to exaggerate and, like the Archer, they fire so many arrows that they can't always see where they land! You throw yourself enthusiastically into one adventure after another, without finishing any of them. You're clumsy around the house and often break things. Your honesty also makes you put your foot in it and blurt out other peoples' secrets. What a girl!

Talents and Hobbies

Sagittarian girls love to study and are excellent at sport and athletics, especially the long jump. You love ski-ing and camping, and you want to travel round the world with nothing but a ruck-sack on your back. You LOVE dogs and horses and always make sure that they get plenty of exercise.

 ## Home and School

A Sagittarian is a messy lass and her room is usually a tip, but as she doesn't spend much time indoors, it doesn't matter! She sticks sport and travel pictures on her walls, and loves purple quilt covers. At school, she's always losing her homework and teachers tell her off for being untidy. Her favourite subjects are geography and P.E., and she's top of the class for popularity with the other girls!

Sagittarius and Boys

You like the energy that boys have and often join in their games. Boys think you are good fun because you organise great parties, and you think up the best games to play. You're a tomboy and refuse to dress up for the sake of a boy. You like to be in a crowd of boys, rather than going steady with just one because you want to be free as a bird. You always have more fun chasing lads than catching them!

The best boys for you are fire signs like yourself, so try an Aries or Leo. They love your sense of adventure. Shy Pisces and Virgo lads make you feel awkward, but if you want to see the world, choose a Libran. He's got the same dreams as you and he'll follow you anywhere!

Sagittarius Girl

Find out how you get on with other starsigns, like your best friend or sister.

Aries the Ram
You both love running about and burning off lots of energy, like mad things. Other people find the pair of you too rough and lively!

Taurus the Bull
Taureans quieten you down but you can feel too stifled by them. You sometimes wish they had more get up and go.

Gemini the Twins
A Gemini always says the opposite thing to you, but you don't mind because you like yakking on about people and places.

Cancer the Crab
You find Cancer too timid and not sporty enough, but you like the way the Crab thinks of you first and tries to understand you.

Leo the Lion
Lions try to push you around, and you just let them think they've got away with it because you always find it easy to make a Leo laugh.

Virgo the Virgin
Virgos are great to have on your side and are full of ideas. They don't mind your showing-off but they're too moany for you sometimes.

Libra the Scales
Librans don't get upset easily which you like, but they do need to be given a push now and then, or you'd both always be stuck indoors.

Scorpio the Scorpion
You are different to them and that's what you like most about Scorpios. They pay you lots of attention and listen carefully to what you say.

Sagittarius the Archer
You both like being outdoors, playing sports or finding the action. You have the same sense of zany humour but others don't get the joke!

Capricorn the Goat
You find the Goat is too serious and snobby for you but you admire the way they always get what they want.

Aquarius the Water Carrier
Aquarians surprise you with their amazing ideas and you find them exciting. You'd like to travel the world together to faraway places.

Pisces the Fishes
You think Pisces is a cry-baby and gets hurt too easily. But they are kind and loving and bring out your studious and sentimental side.

Zodiac Boys

If you get to know a boy's star sign, you'll know whether you'll love him or hate him when he's around.

Aries

He's noisy and quick-tempered, and gets in fights. He's very competitive in sports. He likes girls who crack jokes and answer back.

Taurus

He's slow and often comes last but he loves his food! He can be boring but he wants a girlfriend. Give him sweets, and he's yours!

Gemini

He's cute and always on his bike or skateboard. He goofs around, answers back and argues. Argue back and you'll terrify him!

Cancer

He's shy but friendly, and blushes a lot. He sticks up for girls. He loves his family and pets, and never stops talking about them!

Leo

He's confident and a leader, and he bosses everyone and shows off. He's very popular, because he's the bad lad who every girl wants!

Virgo

He's quiet and studious, but cheeky. He likes clean, tidy girls. He's sarcastic, so don't let him put you down - be rough with him!

Libra
He's gorgeous - and he knows it! He's cool, arty, and likes music and singing. He's a flirt, but he loves clever, lively and forceful girls.

Scorpio
He's competitive, and he tries to make sure he wins! He loves swimming but skives off a lot. He's always trying to snog girls he likes.

Sagittarius
He's good at footie and dreams of travelling the world. He likes girls who make him laugh, but he'll play rotten practical jokes on you!

Capricorn
He's serious and mature. He does well at school and doesn't seem interested in girls. But if you get to know him, he's lovely!

Aquarius
He may be weird-looking but he's warm and friendly, and a computer freak. If you beat him at computer games, he'll notice you fast!

Pisces
He's friendly and chatty. He likes writing and art, and gets crushes on pretty teachers. If you want to be special to him, play hard to get.

Capricorn the Goat

All about Capricorn

Capricorn is the sign of the Goat and there's
nothing a Capricorn girl likes better than a
mountain to climb! She's a big success story
because not only is she ambitious, she's also
willing to work hard to make sure she does
well. If you're a Capricorn, you take life
seriously and like to be in control, so you're
cautious and sensible, and you are so mature
that people think you are older than you are.

You're also interested in history, including your family tree, and that's great, but remember to make the most of the present. You believe in politeness and you tend to stick to the rules, but more than anything, you care about your reputation and you want to do things properly.

Silly Billy!

Capricorn girls can get sad and down about life in general, for no real reason, and they sink into mopey moods and feel as if they have no friends. They hold themselves back and feel they are useless, especially if they experienced unhappy events when they were tiny tots. A Capricorn has to make an effort to look on the bright side and value her positive qualities. You can be a really silly billy goat, too, if you get stuck-up and think someone is beneath you. When you're warm and friendly to others, they are sure to be the same towards you!

Talents and Hobbies

Capricorn girls never waste time and aren't keen on parties. They prefer conversations about important issues. They are more studious than sporty and like reading and hobbies they can do alone, such as photography. They're fascinated by ancient mysteries and love poking around in Aztec calendars and Egyptian hieroglyphics.

Home and School

A Capricorn girl is a good all-rounder but she often prefers science. She always does her homework and doesn't waste time winding up teachers, so she could be a monitor or head girl. At home, she doesn't bother to make her room too pretty, but she does appreciate classy things and her favourite object is a wooden chest of drawers or desk from an aunt or grandparent.

Capricorn and Boys

You're not much fussed about boys because they seem so idiotic, and you don't fall for them often because your head rules your heart. You like older lads and can get a crush on a teacher, especially if he has a beard. Once you find a special boy, you're as giddy as the next girl and you want to go steady and be his one true love. Ah!

The best boys for you are earth signs like yourself, so try a Taurus or Virgo. You feel at ease with them and they admire your determination. You don't feel happy around an angry Aries or a moody Cancer, so if you want true l-u-r-v-e, choose a Pisces boy. He's impossible to control, but he'll lighten you up and show you the funny side of life.

Capricorn Girl

Find out how you get on with other starsigns, like your best friend or sister.

Aries the Ram
You admire their liveliness and sheer cheek, but you don't like going places with the Rams because they show you up.

Taurus the Bull
They make you feel a live-wire, and you nag them to go out more often. But you listen to everything they say about your appearance.

Gemini the Twins
You don't get on because the Twins blow hot and cold, and they think you're telling them off for being trivial.

Cancer the Crab
The Crabs rely on you when they're in a pickle but you wish they wouldn't go on about who does and doesn't love them!

Leo the Lion
You sometimes secretly wish you were a Leo because they seem full of life, but after a while, you realise they're full of themselves!

Virgo the Virgin
They can be your best friends because you're both serious and hard-working. But split up at parties as others don't get your sarky jokes!

Libra the Scales
You're fascinated by Librans' fancy schemes, but you fall out when they break promises and leave you in the lurch.

Scorpio the Scorpion
It takes a long time for you to get to know and trust each other, even years! But then you respect each other's strong will-power.

Sagittarius the Archer
You get embarrassed because they talk loudly and exaggerate their importance. If only they would sit down and shut up sometimes!

Capricorn the Goat
You understand each other but they don't excite you, so you don't put yourself out. Once you're buddies, though, it lasts forever.

Aquarius the Water Carrier
You love to argy-bargy about how to change the world! You like history, but they are futuristic and love gadgets and the space age.

Pisces the Fishes
Their imagination and your ambition make you a perfect match. You bring out the best in each other. Stick together and you'll go far!

Zodiac Friends

What are you like as a friend? What special qualities do you possess that make you popular?

Aries Friends
You are energetic and always enthusiastic. You cheer everyone up as you're so bright and bubbly. Your friends trust you completely.

Taurus Friends
You're reliable, patient and have common sense. Your shoulder is always there for a friend to cry on and you give brilliant advice.

Gemini Friends
You have all the latest gossip and tell the best jokes. Things are never boring when you're around because you know so many fab boys.

Cancer Friends
You are kind, sympathetic and popular. You care about a friend's ups and downs, and you always give exactly the right presents!

Leo Friends
You're generous, warm, and loyal. You always think the best of your friends and when they do well at something, you feel really glad.

Virgo Friends
You happily do anything for your friends and know all their likes and dislikes, and they love it when you take the mickey.

Libra Friends
You enjoy yourself, and you're always smiling. You know what looks good on your friends and you help them look their best.

Scorpio Friends
You're fussy who you befriend and get pally with the strong, smart girls in the class. You expect a lot from them but you also give a lot.

Sagittarius Friends
You're hard to keep up with but you make your friends laugh with your mad goings-on. You also know all the best fun places to visit.

Capricorn Friends
You make long lasting friendships and are always loyal. You see the funny side of things but only share it with other close friends.

Aquarius Friends
You are open and friendly, and are one of the gang. You bring out the best in your mates, appreciating how unique each one is.

Pisces Friends
You are easy to get along with and you make your friends' lives better. You're also wise, and friends ask your help with their problems.

Aquarius the Water Carrier

All About Aquarius

Aquarius is the sign of the Water Carrier, bringing thoughts from the future into the present, and that makes an Aquarian girl a real individual, full of original ideas that are way ahead of her time. She loves her independence and needs to be free and have space in order to be happy and at ease. If you are an Aquarian, you have strong beliefs and you're willing to risk everything if you think you are acting for a good cause.

20th January - 18th February

You like to campaign for people less fortunate than you, and to protect nature, and you believe you can bring changes which make the world a better place. But more than anything, an Aquarian girl is friendly and sociable, and even though she likes to be a bit different, she always wants to be part of the gang.

Whacky Camel

Aquarian girls sometimes take their need to be different too far, and they refuse to dress conventionally or be ordinary, like everyone else. When an Aquarian gets a bee in her bonnet, she's also stubborn and it's almost impossible to budge her. So remember, Aquarius, when you think you are sticking to your principles and you're telling yourself: "I KNOW I'm right", you are almost certainly wrong!

Talents and Hobbies

You have a futuristic imagination, so science and technology attract you. You're inventive and love playing around with CDs and musical equipment, as well as mixing different clothes and colours to create a trendy look. Ultra-modern devices fascinate you, but although you could be a whizz-kid at computer games, they soon bore you.

Home and School

An Aquarian girl loves tuning in to what others are up to, and surfing the Internet or sending e-mails to pen-friends keeps her in touch. At school she only works hard at subjects she enjoys, or if she wants to please a teacher she respects. Her room usually has cool, blue colours, and she prefers blinds to curtains. She never has daft ornaments cluttering it because she likes to feel air and space around her.

Aquarius and Boys

You see everyone as equal and prefer to treat boys and girls the same. Boys are attracted by your genuine, no-nonsense personality, and you like to argue with them and challenge their ideas. You're not bothered about finding a boyfriend and rarely get silly crushes on lads like your friends do.

The best boys for you are air signs like yourself, Gemini and Libra. They're clever and chatty and don't get too heavy. Leos and Scorpios annoy you by being bossy, so a Sagittarius boy suits you best. He's a freedom-lover like you, and he'll make you laugh when you take yourself too seriously.

Aquarius Girl

Find out how you get on with other starsigns, like your best friend or sister.

Aries the Ram
The Ram doesn't like clingy people and that suits you. You're both independent and let each other get on with things.

Taurus the Bull
The Bull calms you down and makes you see things 'normally'. You're both stubborn, so you won't say sorry after an argument.

Gemini the Twins
The Twins always thinks they're right and you love catching them out. You have lots in common and never stop talking.

Cancer the Crab
The Crab gets on your nerves by being soppy or weepy, and you never know WHY. At least you know they care.

Leo the Lion
You sometimes get jealous of the attention the Lions get, but you love their courage and the way they let you know how special you are.

Virgo the Virgin
Virgos are clever with their hands and you admire how careful and neat they are. If only they would stop worrying!

Libra the Scales
You both love art and music but a Libran always agrees with you. It's irritating, until you realise that they want what you want!

Scorpio the Scorpion
You disagree about everything, yet you love a Scorpio's company. But when they go silent or moody, you can't be bothered with them.

Sagittarius the Archer
You love chatting and swapping clothes. You both want freedom but you can get upset when they suddenly go off with other friends.

Capricorn the Goat
The Goat seems old-fashioned but you have many common interests. Make them more adventurous and see how much fun life is.

Aquarius the Water Carrier
You're both friendly and if you're not best mates, you're in the same gang. You enjoy doing things together, like after-school clubs.

Pisces the Fishes
You're both kind and loving, and you often go to the cinema together. But you tease them for really believing what's on the screen!

Pisces the Fishes

All about Pisces

Pisces is the last sign of the Zodiac, and that means a Pisces girl is so considerate of what other people want, she puts herself after everyone else. She's got a heart of gold and loves being helpful when there's a problem to deal with. That's not the whole story because Pisces has TWO fishes, and if you're a Pisces, one half of you is a friendly, helpful dolphin, and the other is a fast, sharp shark.

19th February - 20th March

So you aren't a doormat, and even though you are a gentle dreamer with bags of imagination, you can shock others by being tough and hard. But more than anything, a Pisces is a wise girl who mysteriously knows how others feel, yet because she herself is so deep and subtle, she's always a mystery to them!

Dozy Fish!

Pisces girls are day-dreamers who want to escape from ordinary life. They can be unrealistic and should say 'no' more often, otherwise they bite off more than they can chew, promising things they can't deliver. A Pisces can also be slow on the uptake and get the wrong end of the stick, especially when mates are making arrangements for meeting up. So, Pisces, when you get lost or you're home alone, don't feel sorry for yourself. It was probably YOU who created the muddle in the first place!

Talents and Hobbies

Pisces girls are born actresses who love watching films and videos. They have powerful imaginations and enjoy novels and romantic stories about great heroes and heroines. They write stories, too, but a Piscean likes to drift along, so one of her fave hobbies is sleeping. She's really good at it!

Home and School

A Pisces girl is easy-going and doesn't mind going to school. She even feels OK about wearing a uniform, but she'll skive P.E. Her English teachers love her creative writing but she gets in trouble for punctuality and she's often late. At home, she's got masses of big boy pics on her walls - and masses of dust everywhere else! But her room is warm and comfy, and just the place for a good long chat.

Pisces and Boys

You're such a quiet but strong person that boys can't suss you out, and that makes you mega attractive. You always have at least one boy you fancy (usually two!), and you're a softie who believes everything a boy says. Careful! You are very impressionable and if you get in with the wrong lad, your own personality could get crushed by his.

The best boys for you are water signs like yourself, Cancer and Scorpio. You can share all your thoughts with them, and they can cope with your emotional ups and downs. You feel threatened by racy Gemini or Leo lads, so if you want a boy who cares, choose a Capricorn. He takes ages to get close but when he does, he's a friend for life.

Pisces Girl

Find out how you get on with other starsigns, like your best friend or sister.

Aries the Ram
You love being with the Rams because they are always up to something new, and they like you because you make them feel talented.

Taurus the Bull
The Bull brings out your bossy streak and you're always forcing them into having new experiences.

Gemini the Twins
You're not close to the Twins but you like their jokes and songs, and they bring you out of yourself and make you talk.

Cancer the Crab
You and the Crab are both from the sea, so you love paddling along together, gossiping about everyone's secrets. Sshh!

Leo the Lion
You envy them because they've got so much going for them, but you find them too big-headed when they tell you how brill they are.

Virgo the Virgin
You're totally different but you're both perfectionists who fuss over school projects and look after animals together.

Libra the Scales
You like the way a Libran makes you think for yourself but you get confused when they say one thing and then do something else!

Scorpio the Scorpio
You like each other a lot and gossip about everything. But be careful that they don't use you in their plans to get revenge on someone!

Sagittarius the Archer
They strut around wanting to know why you aren't doing this or that. You think they hurt people's feelings too much, especially yours!

Capricorn the Goat
You like them because they treat you well and you know where you stand with them. They never let you down and tell you their secrets.

Aquarius the Water Carrier
You're good friends but you get touchy with each other, especially when you blurt out a secret and embarrass them!

Pisces the Fishes
Don't spend too much time together! You are both vague and muddled, swimming around in circles and going nowhere!